Johnfrmunro@yahoo.co.uk

Follow the author at:

https://twitter.com/johnfrmunro

Editing and Cover by Sam McGurran

https://sammcgurran.com/

In Association with the Gorbals Writing Group

https://gorbalswrites.wordpress.com/

https://www.facebook.com/gorbalswrites/

ISBN: 9781697449518 First Edition

By John FR Munro

Short Stories and Poems

Essentary

This book is dedicated to my wife, my family and my friends.

Acknowledgements

I'd like to thank Sam McGurran (Writer, Poet, Editor - AKA the Man who Can) for all his help in editing and getting my ideas into a proper book.

I'm eternally grateful to all the Guest Writers for offering their writing to this book, their continued creative support and for being there with me during my journey from procrastination to publication.

"The Gift" was performed on stage in London on the 17th December 2018 and without the talent and support of Simon Fisher (Simon Fisher, theatre and film writer/director and Director of The Gift) and Shane Noone (Poet, Writer and Actor - including the monologue for The Gift) and Heather Ward (Artistic Director and Producer) and her phenomenal team of creative geniuses at Directors Cut Theatre Company

I continue to be inspired by members of KITC (Kick In The Creatives) and the artistic genius of "In Search of Faerie Nuff".

Finally, my thanks go to all those who have supported me and the Gorbals Writing Group; this includes Micheal Fullerton (Thriving Places); Roz Adams (Bridging The Gap) and all the Gorbals Library staff.

Essentary

by John FR Munro

CONTENTS

THE GIFT

Mark looked at his tattooed arm
The Regimental crest, his good luck charm
His children's names he gave a stroke
What happened to that army bloke?

He washed himself from head to toe
He had to be quick, so no one would know
He used various toilets for the disabled
People like him were quickly labelled

Dosser, tosser, homeless scum,
vagrant, tramp and even bum.
He served his country with courage and pride.
No one knew how he felt inside.

For two years he'd slept beneath the sky,
as angry people passed him by.
Pointing, shouting, hurling abuse.
His baggy clothing hanging loose.

His muscles were almost worn away
Though he tried to exercise each day
But people mocked and moved him on
Street living's no fun, down in London

That Christmas Eve he hunkered down,
in his alley he saw the McDonalds clown.
Cardboard boxes 'neath his clothes
Above him snow, upon his nose.

His balaclava covered his face,
but in his heart he felt disgrace.
How had he succumbed to PTSD
"Is this God's way of testing me?"

He felt himself drift into sleep,

the snow now lying, inches deep.
Tremors ran throughout his skin.
This happens when you're really thin.

He heard a crunch upon the snow
And a voice that said, "here's one to go"
He felt himself picked from the floor.
They were five, maybe more.

He felt himself move into light.
So, he thought, I die tonight.
Voices swirled, inside his head
Something about "Big Red"

Hours later he awoke
He was in a bed. Is this a joke?
A room so happy, warm and clean
So different from his normal routine

He slowly raised his body up
Saw a kettle, coffee and a cup
An envelope with MARK was plain to see
Who was sending mail to me?

He opened it up and read it fast
And then again, to make it last
"We are the Secret Santa Society,
Who've all suffered pain and PTSD"

"You're in a hotel, for the week,
Reception will call us if you want to speak
You are under no obligation
To speak to us about your situation"

"We'd love to help, as others helped us,
You probably don't want to cause a fuss
We can help you, but it's up to you,
So what, would you like to do?"

Mark started crying, tears hit the page
He felt like he'd been released from a cage
Time to get back on his feet
Time not to wallow in defeat

He looked out the window, the world was all white
The world had turned to day from night
Today was a new start, he knew what to do
The phone was answered with "How can I help you?"

INSIDE

I know it's mine,
But it's hard to define,
Through the tears that I've cried,
It still stays, inside

There's a million bits to my heart,
And you touched every part
There are things, I left unspoken
My heart a jigsaw that now lies broken

Though I scream and I shout,
The pain won't come out.
Though I know that you've died,
I still feel you, inside.

SOMETHING COLD

I'm sitting eating all alone
No happy ringtone on my phone
I've something that I need to say
"Again, I forgot our Anniversary"

My beloved has just gone out
She didn't speak, swear or shout
Instead, she's giving me the cold shoulder
I should know better, I have got older

She's going drinking with her mate
She'll be back drunk, it will be late
I better sleep in the spare room
Beside the hoover and the broom

I climb the stairs and open the door
She's hid the bed, there's only floor
I go to find it in the cellar
The door's locked, she hates her feller

No blankets or duvet to be found
I guess I'm sleeping on the ground
The floor is cold, I'm learning a lesson
Forgetting her equals a lack of compassion

FIGHTING LIKE CATS AND DOGS

Barron, apart from being a lovable dog, was also the self-proclaimed King of his Castle. Well, at least the King of Castle Street, where he lived with his owner Kevin.

There had been many who had tried to oppose his magnificent rule, all had failed - miserably.

Most recently, it had been the dreadful Russian woman. Svetlana. The "Cussing Cossack", the "Vulgar from the Volga", with her beast eyes, nose warts and ever so skinny sausage dog - Smelly Sergei.

Barron had successfully ousted them both from his kingdom due to his ninja-like skills and implementation of Carpetgate. (Carefully placing pieces of chewed up rug from the living room into the quilted basket of Sergei, had been worthy of any spy dog novel.)

Memories of her denials and the dirty looks from her dog, as they left with suitcases of assorted clutter, made him smile. When they left in the taxi, he broke into his "I like to move it, move it" dance.To this day, his recurring regret was that it had not been recorded and submitted to his favourite TV show "Dogs Have Talent"

After a year of enduring his masters sensibility, sobriety, secrecy, serenity and morose silence, Barron awoke to the unexpected knowledge of Kevin having acquired a skip to his step, a song in his heart, a reason for whistling out of tune.

Kevin had a new amour.

Barron had grudgingly accepted that the hours his master spent on dating apps would eventually result in a match; he'd just hoped that it would take longer.

Following an eternity of mobile phone calls, with "you hang up, no you hang up" she finally made an appearance and was now starting to come round a little too often for his liking

Barrons' first impressions were that she was a cheap, perfume-bathing, lipstick applying, rouge wearing, eyelash fluttering, high-heel clattering, nonstop nattering, wine drinking, garlic eating, French floozy.

Alternatively she went by the name of 'Parisa'

The animals in the street didn't risk asking Barron for second impressions, as he had very strict rules regarding first impressions and no one wanted to spend hours hearing him recite them

Kevin was now busy spending copious amounts of time in front of his bedroom mirror practicing how to say "Ooh La La" and "Oui"

Barron knew things were going wrong when he overheard them having an unsettling settee conversation; whilst allegedly enjoying mixed vegetables and a very smelly Camembert cheese fondue(which in itself, constituted an environmental health risk).

The following words raised red flags to his delicate ears

"Diet"
"Exercise regime"
"Fido"
"Trip to Paris"
"Synergy of cats and dogs cohabitation is healthy for the well-being of evolution and of course the balance of the planet"

Barron's worst fears were realised later that lazy Sunday afternoon, during the Antiques Road Show, when Kevin turned to the French folly and said

"OK. Let's give moving in together a go; I'm sure things will be fine."

Barron lay there with droopy eyes, a heavy heart and empty stomach, vowing to vanquish this new enemy

———

In the cat world, the Persian is the glamor puss.
With a beautiful, glowing, flowing coat, sweet face and calm

personality, this combination makes them the most popular cat breed.

When in fact they're the Devils Disciples.

Though they are universally renowned as being very high maintenance and even though they have some health issues - sadly - humans continue to overlook these matters.

For many their looks and personality overcome those drawbacks.

Melodi, loved being a Persian as much as being the centre of attention. Those who knew her - including her friends - would say "there's nothing nice about her as she's a self-absorbed egotistical feline fantasist."

When she heard she was moving from her palatial apartment overlooking the River Thames to some grubby basement flat, she was decidedly unimpressed.

In reality she was moving from a block of council flats to a nicer area but just didn't know it, or appreciate it.

Her horror at the news of living with a dog was evident in her words, "the day the world ACTUALLY stopped."

Melodi was also prone to exaggeration and being staggeringly overdramatic.

———

Parisa and Melodi arrived in style to the bemusement of the various animal residents of Castle Street.

It wasn't every day you got to see a limousine arrive and witness about 20 assorted suitcases and designer bags being carried into the basement flat of the young man who didn't appear to own a comb or hairbrush.

In neighbouring homes, the local cats, dogs and Pedro the Parrot all noted the arrival of the Persian and within an hour of her arrival they'd met up to bet on how long she would survive living in Castle Street with Barron.

Sean the Irish wolfhound (and local bookie), took his first bets from Haggis the Dandie Dinmont and Aggie the Skye Terrier.

Haggis and Aggie had a polite nodding acceptance of each other and Sean was surprised that they'd both said "The Persian will rule the roost in that house."

Pedro the Parrot, who lived with Mr Potter, was undecided, but Barron had support from old Clement the Basset Hound and Midas the Golden Retriever.

The three female cats who lived in the street; Abby, Gloria and Trixie, all bet on the new girl. They knew a gold digger when they saw one

Sean declined the offering of a freshly caught mouse from Magnus, the scruffy, the smelly cat from number 7, as it was actually a hamster and belonged to the wee girl at number 11. Magnus was told to return it and bring a proper treat as the bet.

Magnus huffed and puffed his way back to number 11 and decided to sit this one out, based on the fact he'd eaten all his other treats.

Humans are often so absorbed in their own happiness that they "forget the pet" and in a social media world, the habit of writing things down is sadly becoming a thing of the past.

These are the jottings of Barron and Parisa. Yeah

DOG DAY DIARY - Day 1

Not a good day, apparently a diet is a French humans idea of torture.

Miss Froggy thinks that my chubbiness and cuddliness, nurtured over many a year isn't cute

It's a pity that the Fat Cat isn't on a diet, as Melodi the "Devils Daughter" is now marking her territory, as only a stinky cat, can.

Mr Potter wasn't feeling very well and Kevin had popped in to see how his neighbour was doing and fed Pedro the Parrot who lives with Mr Potter.

CAT CHRONICLES - Day 1

Dear World, please save me from this intolerable tragedy.

The Male human of the house is just weird and speaks to me in some version of what he thinks is French and appears to know a Parrot called Pedro

The enormous smelly lump of hair in the corner of the room is apparently called Barron. I'm now spraying the house to remove the smell of dog

My mistress seems to be giggling a lot; I think she might be having another one of her episodes.

DOG DAY DIARY - Day 2

OMG - Why has no one ever designed gas masks for dogs?

Where does this cat find all the putrid liquid she's spraying the house with?

A machine arrived today called "F1DO" it's a FEED 1 DOG ONLY device, that was obviously something Torquemada the Torturer invented

The device operates by my paw being recognised and providing sustenance

I assume that it's malfunctioning or it must have various settings and the dog setting selected must be for a bloody Chihuahua

I am STARVING.

CAT CHRONICLES - Day 2

The hairy lump never stops moaning.

The humans are practicing how to do a proper French kiss.

A lot of much needed practice is now going on, as apparently his imbecilic technique is like being probed at the dentist and he might have loosened one of her fillings. My mistress's words not mine.

The constant sound of slurping is very distressing and is akin to a young child with its first ice cream. Or a hoover that has somehow got a beach ball stick on the tube thing. My words not hers.

The dog continues to suffer his diet, which has been the highlight of my day.

The neighbours appear to be a strange lot, especially the Parrot.

———

DOG DAY DIARY - Day 3

I have been informed that Red Cross parcels are always welcomed by the humans, is there an animal equivalent?

I'd settle for a slice of pizza being poked through the letter box

My paws are too big to dial the RSPCA

The humans have bizarrely started to wear matching clothes; my master has for some reason taken to wearing a blue and white jumper and a beret

A string of onions that he bought has helped disguise Parisa's "Petsonal" Pee Perfume

She's taken to burying my toys in the garden, like some demonic pirate

———

CAT CHRONICLES - Day 3

Bored.
Bored.
BORED.
Burying Barrons stuff because I'm so very bored.
Humans are now dressing like a mime act.
Neighbours are strange; they just sit and watch Barron and me.

Weird.

———

DOG DAY DIARY - Day 4

Yes

Yes

YES

Ate my food, stole the cats food, got a treat from the street when a drunk guy who dropped some chips

Sprinkled itching powder into the cat basket of Smug Puss, she's not looking happy

————

CAT CHRONICLES - Day 4

Call in the hostage rescue team.
My mistress must think I need to go on a diet, she has left me no food.
The lack of food has had an immediate effect on me.
I can't stop scratching myself.

———

DOG DAY DIARY - Day 5

Getting up early to steal the cats food is fun

The humans are talking about a trip to France and a thing called "Kennels".

———

CAT CHRONICLES - Day 5

No food AGAIN.
Everything is spinning; I can't find the strength to walk.
Dear World, FAREWELL.

———

DOG DAY DIARY - Day 6

I now know what a Kennel is.

Aaaaaaaaaggggghh!

I need to get Fat Cat on my side.

But I've eaten her food.

I've offered her my food as she seems to be very listless.

———

CAT CHRONICLES - Day 6

Barron has saved my life.
He has selflessly sacrificed his own food to keep me alive.
I am indebted to him, forever.
Barron has advised me of the Killer Kennels of Kensington, we must join forces.

———

DOG DAY DIARY - Day 7

We have a plan.

Can't share humans are watching us.

———

CAT CHRONICLES - Day 7

Barron thinks he has a plan.
I think we need more cunning and Barron is as sharp as a space hopper.
I have a very cunning plan.

———

DOG DAY DIARY - Day 8

Parisa has given me some subtle clues as to how we overcome the

Kennel situation.

She thinks that I don't know that she's manipulating me, but if she'd just be open and honest I wouldn't have had to terrorise her with the fabricated stories of incarceration.

The plan is being put into action today.

———

CAT CHRONICLES - Day 8

I've just stolen their passports.
Barron has hidden them.
The humans are looking for them.
There's a continued mention of "cat burglars" so I'm keeping my head down.

———

CAT CHRONICLES - Day 9

The animals in the street have stopped watching us.

Apparently Pedro was recently given a load of treats for saying "we deserve each other".

Not sure if that's worthy of lots of treats but the fact Pedro shared them with Barron and myself was kinda nice.

LANDSCAPE

If I was living on the moon
I'd be shouting floods are coming soon,
act now to save the Earth,
but what is my opinion worth?

Before my eyes, the tides would rise,
How can they even act surprised?
What more do I have to say,
It's creeping closer, day by day.

The seas will rise from east to west,
Will we learn to share the rest?
Or can we work to avert this tragedy
Let's work to save it, who is with me?

LOST SOULS

I awoke to what sounded like breaking glass. Not a single smash, but a series of very different glass smashing noises.

If I were a sound technician - which I'm not - I'd have said some were maybe drinking glasses, a few like windows and one resembled a picture frame.

I hoped that I'd left the television on and a late night film was to blame and crossed my fingers that I wasn't being burgled.

In polite society, it's always considered a good idea to introduce yourself at the beginning of a tale.

So I apologise for skipping that bit.

My name is Amenadiel D'Angelo and my friends call me Amen.

For some reason I have just been chosen to be involved in something called Project Prism, but I'll get to that soon.

But, back to the sound of breaking glass. Not being a slippers kind of guy, I slowly took the stairs in the dark, making mental notes to fix the squeaky bits.

I was wearing an old t-shirt and a pair of shorts. Neither of which were particularly clean or trendy, which enhanced my embarrassment when I arrived in my living room to see a young, beautiful, leather-clad brunette reclining on a bright-red, shiny Harley Davidson motorcycle.

She appeared to be drinking the last of my tequila from the bottle and had thrown books from my small library at various glass objects.

In my head, I heard her speak.

Oh My Demons. She broke into throaty laughter. *Well no wonder you sleep alone stud.*

Her perfectly formed bright red lips did not move, yet I could clearly hear her in my brain.

What's the bedside lamp for? She laughed again. *Are you the light infantry?*

I continued to cling onto the lamp I'd brought for protection and wished I had so many really great comebacks.

Instead, I found myself thinking. Wow. She's stunning.

My next thoughts were.

Who are you?

Why are you here?

Why are you destroying my stuff?

How did you get a motorcycle into my house without me hearing anything?

Are you single?

She smiled and proceeded to silently rattle off answers to all my questions straight into my brain

I'm Lucy, my boss sent me, I was trying to get your attention, my boss is Lucifer and we get to do wonderfully strange stuff.

This is my latest fun idea; I don't speak as I'm playing 'mind games'.

Oh and you've no chance of asking me out, so please close your mouth, that cartoon open jaw look, really doesn't suit you.

I took a step forward and suddenly found myself flying through the air and landing on my sofa.

She blew me a kiss.

Relax, I'm here to deliver an invitation.

Trying to act cool, I silently replied,

"*And if I refuse?*"

She laughed maniacally,

Well, I suppose there has to be a first time, but I wouldn't recommend it. So, hear me out.

"I'm all ears" I said sarcastically.

That can be arranged, so choose your words carefully, her voice purred in my head.

A purple envelope floated over to me and inside was a black invitation card with red trim and white writing; it was brief, intriguing and utterly terrifying.

YOU ARE INVITED TO VISIT HELL, FOR A 24 HOUR SHOW AND TELL.

I tried to stop various things going through my mind, knowing that Lucy knew what I was thinking, but you try not thinking.

She responded quickly,
Firstly - I've no idea why you've been chosen, but I must say that you do have a very interesting first name.
Secondly- You're not on my list for dispatching or collecting so you're safe, for now.
Thirdly- it's not a test, well not that I'm aware of.
Finally- There's no need to wear fireproof clothing.

I ever so slightly nodded my head, which she mistakenly took as agreement as opposed to an acknowledgement and I suddenly found myself in a large hangar.

The first things I noticed were; I wasn't wearing the same clothes and Lucy was laughing in my head. The expression wicked sense of humour came to mind.

Lucy cupped my elbow and directed me to a room that read BITCH(Basic Induction Training Centre Hell).

As I waited, I examined my pink jumpsuit with Unicorns, fluffy rainbow slippers, sparkly bum bag and jester's hat.

I didn't ask why, I was pretty sure I didn't want to know the answer.

The induction was carried out by the world's most boring man and the clock behind him never moved, despite the agony going on for at least an hour.

After half an hour, a woman walked in with a trolley full of tea, coffee and beautiful sandwiches, cakes, scones, jam and clotted cream. She swiftly circled the room and left before I could get anything.

The next phase was site orientation and I noticed a few specific things about the hanger.

There was not a sound, despite a massive queue of people in all sorts of conditions and lots of them were holding things, like bags, umbrellas, parachutes, life preservers, backpacks, bikes and suitcases

There was a large sign saying BAGGAGE over an empty area.

A neon sign was flashing above a selection of poster boards one minute it had 'HAHA' in bright RED then it read 'Heaven And Hell Aligned' but only for a few seconds and it was in a flashing BRIGHT WHITE.

On one of the boards there were a selection of before and after pictures.

One that stood out was a picture of a rose tattooed on a shapely firm buttock with a post-it above the picture saying 2012 and right beside it was the same image that now looked like a cabbage on a very flabby buttock with 2019 above it

A board with SUICIDE on it had a map of the world with various graphs and pie charts showing data gathered.

I noticed a pin in a circle around the UK and Republic of Ireland with a piece of glittery string leading to another pin holding a piece of paper in place.

I read:

2017 - Total 6,213 suicides

2017 - Republic of Ireland - 392 suicides

2017 - UK - 5,821 suicides

2017 - 71 military suicides

Suicide remains the most common cause of death for men aged 20-49.

My eyes filled with tears.

A klaxon sounded and the queue moved forward one person at a time, to a table where an old white bearded man sat sleeping, or at least he appeared to be.

No words were being exchanged, occasionally there would be some animations from the person stepping forward, but they'd sadly trudge make their way to the back of the queue and slowly shuffle forward to the front.

The queue was orderly and at the front of the queue was a yellow line that no one crossed till the klaxon sounded

I noticed LUCY watching me and got her attention with a thought. "*Is this it?*"

She escorted me into a room where a large plasma screen showed me a devilishly good looking man sitting by the sea.

He turned and smiled, his voice both menacing and intoxicating in my head,

"I've taken the day off, thanks to you"

I went to speak but my tongue was stuck to the top of my mouth. **"Amen, you've no idea yet, who you are. Do you?"**

I found myself involuntarily shaking my head. "*No.*"

"Every one hundred years, you are reborn at exactly one second into the new year. Yes 2000 was another good year and I get to convince you to join me before you're 21. We do it every one hundred years and have recently decided to call it Project Prism, which is quite catchy"

A shiver ran down my spine.

"We are related, irreversibly linked like two sides of a coin and if you choose to join me, we can do marvellous things. I've now got idiots running countries, the environment is being destroyed by the day, plus war and famine are doing great things. I've got flooding and pestilence lined up for this century, you really don't want to miss out on all the good stuff."

I was horrified by his candour, but just couldn't help myself; I was keen to know what the alternatives were.

He interrupted my thoughts.

"You become an Angel and do great things and die just before midnight on the 31st December 2099"

And I mused, so I'm here today because...

"With you there I get a day off. Lucy will look after you"

I wracked my brain for the right thing to say and I had a question.

He got there first.

"Enjoy your visit and I know you're intrigued to know about the BAGGAGE sign, it's for emotional baggage but no one ever leaves any so they stay in the queue till they do, but they're LOST SOULS

so that's not going to happen"

So, here I am - back home - after the worst and weirdest 24 hours of my life, thus far. No angelic job offers yet, so I'm still at university.

Apparently I've to expect a visit from the other side before I am 21, if the world hasn't destroyed itself first.

UNTOLD STORIES

Hush, hush whisper who dares,
The body of my partner, is under the stairs
The silence is deafening, no smashing of things.
It's amazing the happiness, solitude brings.

They said that they loved me
They promised they'd care
Then beat me, abused me
Dragged me, by my hair

Checking my texts, every day
Always careful, of what I might say
Make sure everything's just right
Always afraid of starting a fight

Table set the way they said
Or you're sleeping on the floor instead
Don't open the post,
Don't burn the toast

Making soft boiled eggs is my hell
They'll smash the wrong ones and start to yell
Constantly derided
Confidence eroded

Covering bruises and welts
Delivered, via punches and belts
I'm tragically thin
I'm always locked in

I needed fresh air and a break
Which led to my mistake
I went beyond the back door
And they lost it, once more

They stamped on my bare feet

And started to beat
Everywhere but my face
As that may leave a trace

Of my humiliation
My degradation
As I lay on the floor
The blood started to pour

They stopped for a drink
By the new kitchen sink
As I lay there and cried
An anger, built up inside

They could see I was beat
As I rose to my feet
With their smirk and evil eyes
They were in for a surprise

I saw the bread knife
I thought, save your life
A red mist descended
And in seconds, their life ended

As I view the pool of blood
My trickling tears, become a flood
It seems to take forever
To hide them 'neath the stairs

I'm now sitting, waiting, drinking tea
For someone to scold or arrest me
I expect the police, who knows
To take evidence. My clothes

So please take me, I'm ready
Though my legs are not steady
I'll not raise a single peep
For the first time in ages, I'll get a safe sleep

BRAVEHOUND

I've only known him for a week,
My new best friend who doesn't speak,
Following me wherever I go,
Quietly listening to my tales of woe.

My home was quiet, till he came,
No fun, no laughter, what a shame,
Full of anger, bitterness and gloom,
Despair, residing in every room,

I'd often sit up late at night,
Afraid to turn off any light,
Constantly thinking, constantly drinking,
My self-belief was slowly sinking.

My home was in need of some repair,
A little bit of loving care
A tidy up, a lick of paint,
To take it back to looking quaint

My new best friend's look would harden
At the disaster that was my garden
Instead of lush, green grass
It was a rubbish tip, with broken glass

With big brown eyes and shaggy hair,
He'll often give a loving stare,
Helping me keep my feet on the ground,
All courtesy of Bravehound

A charity, doing the best it can,
To help me as a forces veteran,
Without their help, I'd not be here
My wee dog's brought me lots of cheer

I'm slowing taking back my life,
I'm acknowledging hope, instead of strife,
300 million smell receptors in his nose
When I get anxious, my new friend knows

He cuddles in, when I want to talk,
Fetches his lead to take me for a walk,
If I'm feeling better than yesterday,
Then I'm winning my battle, day by day.

CHEER

"3 cheers for Billy" I hear them say,
Then comes, the first "hip hip hooray"
The second comes and then the third,
The whole thing really is absurd

I no longer have employment,
I'm forced to seek mundane enjoyment,
"Take up bowls and go fishing"
As others are gleefully wishing

But I loved being a member of society,
I don't want pity or sympathy
I'm used to rising with the lark,
I'm not for sitting myself in the park

Watching as the world slowly drifts by,
I feel the tears well up in my eyes
As the cheerers leave the room,
I find myself alone, with my gloom..

THE SUIT

"A 3 piece with a shirt and tie"
I hear her dulcet tones cry,
As I close the door to the conversation,
And go to the pub for a pint of salvation.

"Get a new suit, for my pal's big day"
"It's her 3rd wedding" I'd love to say
"How many more times must she take?
Unless she's addicted to wedding cake"

I'm having a pint, when Bill pops in
Orders a pint and a tonic with gin
"Is that you on the scented stuff?"
He barely smiles, he's in a huff

"You going to the wedding?" he said
I take a drink and nod my head
"I've to get a suit, she's coming in"
So that's why, he's bought a gin

"I'm also heading in, to get a suit,
It's gonna cost me a lotta loot,
I've got a black one, I've worn it once,
What's the point of all the expense?"

Bill nods his head, "I agree with you,
I've got a blue one, it's brand new"
A light bulb flickers above my head,
Maybe we could swap instead

Two hour later, we're in the pub
Having some drinks and a spot of grub
The wives walk in, scowls on their face
"Been looking for you, all over the place"

Safety in numbers, we state our case,
Looking for a smile, to crack their face,
"We've both got a new suit and saved cash,
To treat you at this wedding bash"

The women whisper to each other
Which usually means, someone's in bother
"We've decided, this is what we think,
You can buy us new outfits and a drink."

TM

TM looked through the bars he had taken sanctuary behind and sighed.

He'd done his best, fought a great fight, but he needed to rest. He'd called in reinforcements but they were at least an hour away.

Quiet;y, he sipped water from a small bottle and had a small piece of chocolate to raise his sugar levels.

He could hear them coming, their footsteps pounding, high pitched screeching and screaming filled the air. He sent a text to the incoming rescuer "Save yourself!"

"We're coming to get you" was the threat from a female voice, quickly followed by two others as they baying in unison.

"We're coming to get you, we're coming to get you."

TM wished he'd taken better cover, and used his camouflage skills from the military to greater effect.

The rumbling of feet got louder, his mind was in a whirl, and his heart was racing as they entered the room.

"Tickle Monster, why are you sitting in the play pen" asked his grandchildren as a text came in on his phone,

"You've only watched the weans for an hour, stop being such a drama queen."

SONG

Imagine your life without a song,
Nothing, encapsulating right or wrong,
No communication of celebration,
Desperation or elation.

Just silence or your beating heart
With passion you're dying to impart
No waving arms or dancing feet
Or skipping gaily down the street

Those treasured moments in the arms
Of those you love, with scented charms
No foxtrot, rhumba or even Tango
Where will all that chemistry go?

Think about your favourite song today,
That'll have you on your knees and say
"This is what epitomises me,
nourishes my soul and sets me free."

TIME

Two women waiting for a bus.
One says "He doesn't cause a fuss"
The other "Oh that's good to hear,
Mines going deaf, but in one ear"

The first one pipes up "Mines OK,
I often let him out the back to play"
The second comments "I'll try that out,
But to bring him in, d'you need to shout?"

"I usually yell, it's time for grub,
If he's good, I'll walk him to the pub"
The second lady shakes her head,
"Mine has his food and goes to bed"

I interrupt as nosey folk do,
"I apologise for interrupting you,
Walk kind of dogs d'you both own"
"Husbands" they say, with a frown.

FAVOURITE DECADE

OK. So the 70's just win it
But the 60's was definitely in it
Motown, the sound of Philadelphia
Made me "get on down" and shout "Yeah!"

Yes we had our trouble and strife
But I found myself a wife
I met her over in Germany
I kid myself - she was stalking me

People shared and people cared
Things blown up, were soon repaired
We started on the road to parity,
We now have Equality and Diversity

A night out didn't cost the Earth
Scotland in a World Cup, for what it's worth
My daughter born, in 78
My son in 82, (he turned up late)

Work was hard, yes it was a grind
Today a grind, is shaking your behind
so working your arse off is not the same
If you missed the 70's that's a shame.

DREAM JOB

As I approached the front door of Dads house I was carrying a newspaper, two coffees on a cardboard gizmo, two bacon rolls in paper bags and a bag of sugared donuts

My keys for his house were in my pocket so yet again I kicked the metal letter box at the bottom of the door.

After five attempts and no responses I put everything down, got my keys and opened the door to find the mail not on the door mat. Scooping up the breakfast, calling out

"It's me, your one and only son bringing you a Red Cross parcel from Greggs the Bakers."

I heard a voice from upstairs, "I'm busy up here!" I put everything down and ate my roll and drank my coffee.

He joined me minutes later and he seemed to be in a good mood. We started chatting about last night's football as we had our breakfast.

While I was reading the paper he made his way back upstairs and it was a good ten minutes before I realised he hadn't come back. I went to check on him and took the stairs, clutching the polished wooden bannister as my arthritis played up, yet again.

As I walked into his bedroom, I saw Dad standing in front of a three piece black suit hung up on a wardrobe door, holding two very old ties.

One was a conservative silvery grey and the other, a bright pink.

"Wow, you'd be able to see the pink one from the international space station" I joked.

"I've got two celebrations to attend tonight and I need both" he replied, with a smile.

"You're eighty next week and you've two parties to attend on the same night? That requires the wearing of two very different ties? How did that happen, Mr Popular?"

"Put the kettle on son and I'll tell you all about it." He laid both ties out neatly on the bed and shuffled out of the room.

Five minutes later, we were sat at the kitchen table with mugs of tea and a packet of digestive biscuits.   Taking a biscuit, he broke it in two and held up both bits, "What do I always say?"

"Where's my phone."

"I'm being serious" he said, waving the biscuits

"A promise kept."

"Exactly!" he said, smiling "and tonight I'm keeping a promise I made 50 years ago"

I sat back in my chair, "Wow. I'd have been 5."

"Indeed you were and I was working as a registrar, conducting wedding ceremonies"

Taking another biscuit, dunking it as was my habit, I enquired "So, is this a wee reunion tonight. Are you meeting up with your former Hatch, Match and Dispatch colleagues?"

"Births, Marriages and Deaths, if you don't mind. It's a very responsible role in life. My name and signature will be on documents for centuries to come"

I smiled at the reprimand, knowing he enjoyed the opportunity to regale in his former glory. "And don't forget Dad, you used ink in a fountain pen, that's proper old school"

"That ink was designed to last over one hundred years, now that's technology to be proud of."

"The ties Dad, can you tell me about the ties?"

Putting down the two bits of biscuits he began his tale, "Back in the day, I had a good luck routine for my wedding ceremonies, I'd ask them to choose a tie from my collection to match their ceremony."

"Spot you with the collection. Exactly how many ties did you have?"

"Six, but I only used five for weddings, the black one was for funerals."

"So, what other colours did you have?"

"The gold one was very popular, but it's looking a bit tatty now. I had a red one and a maroon one. It wasn't a good idea to have a blue or a green one, not in this city"

"Well that now explains the two ties on your bed, but how's that relevant to the two events tonight?"

"It started off as a throwaway line, when chatting to the happy couple on their big day" he picked up half a biscuit and dunked it in his near cold tea, which was part of his tea drinking routine

"Go on?"

"All I said was, I'll see you at your golden wedding anniversary."

"You're bloody kidding me!" I laughed.

"The office forwarded onto me two invitations to upcoming 50th wedding celebrations and I'm honour bound to accept and attend."

"You are bloody kidding me!"

"You've already said that," he sniffed.

"No, I mean you're bloody kidding me you remember what ties you wore to those weddings, fifty years ago?"

"Son, it was my dream job and I plan to enjoy remembering every wee bit of it, for as long as I can."

WHISTLE

I heard a whistle in a dream,
I was on a train, propelled by steam,
The carriages were old and cold,
With various markings, of tales untold.

The dent in a door frame,
Was a crying shame,
Was this the result of a trolly?
A lover's dalliance, tragedy or folly?

Scuffed carpet, worn leather seat,
Champagne to drink, canapés to eat
Where a murder would cause distress?
Is this the infamous, Orient Express?

The shrill whistle blew again,
I felt the shaking of the train
And woke to see my angry mother
"The kettles boiled, why do I bother!"

VALUING LIFE

I am a mother and a wife,
I'd sacrifice all, to save my babies life,
I have no food and heat burns up the air,
Another drought, will someone care?

No water, to cool his body down,
I don't think I'll make it into town,
The road is long, full of dust and dirt,
You'd do the same, if your baby was hurt.

Your empathy, your sympathy,
I don't care what you offer me,
Take action now and save a life,
Don't leave me simply as a wife.

CHRISTMAS EVE

Ben set the table on Christmas Eve,
For his wife Mary and best friends, Paul and Steve.
His daughter stood watching, she smiled and said,
"Mum will be delighted, that the tables been laid"

He opened the wine and poured a wee glass,
He asked his daughter "D'you want some, lass?"
Smiling sweetly, she said "no thanks,
I've got stuff to do;
I see you've not lost the ability to use a corkscrew"

She gazed at all the Christmas cards he'd been sent,
Slowly taking the stairs, to wrap his present,
He poured a glass of the fine Malbec,
Then hobbled to his sofa, to take a wee break.

His eyes grew tired; he put down his glass,
I can't spill the wine and upset me lass,
He seemed to drift off, to a wee dozy sleep,
His breathing was shallow, his sleep it was deep

But he jumped, as he heard his doorbell ring,
Broke into a grin, as he heard no carollers sing
The door flew open, the old guys strolled in
Followed by his wife, with a bottle of gin

He shook hands, hugged and then kissed his wife,
A bonny wee lass that he'd known for all his life,
He served them all drinks, then plied them with food,
They chatted and laughed and shared good Christmas mood.

Their dirty, raucous laughter filled the room,
They told tales of fun, not of doom and gloom,
The grandfather clock, struck the first of its ten,
In unison, the 3 asked "Well are you coming out Ben?"

Every Christmas, he nodded his usual "No",
But, this time he decided he wanted to go,
He stood up and said on the tenth chime,
"You know what; I think I'll go with you, this time"

The four all stood up and strode out into the night,
The winters stars above them, twinkled and shone bright,
The moon was full and lit up the sky
All four were laughing with a twinkle in their eye.

The house was too silent, thought the young lass,
Then she heard it, the breaking of glass,
She ran downstairs and saw her dad,
He was lying back, silent, but not looking sad,

She checked his pulse, there wasn't a beat
The red wine and glass now lay at his feet,
She kissed his head and wiped away her tears,
They'd come to get him at last, after all these years.

She straightened her father's one and only tie,
You have to look your best on the day that you die.
She sorted his hair, and put in his cap,
He just looked like he'd been working and was taking a nap.

At Christmas, for years, he'd set the table for four,
A nice glass of Malbec, he would always pour,
With his friends and her mum, they were together at last,
They'd be up in heaven now, having a blast.

MY TIME

My sands of time are swiftly pouring,
I can't waste what's left, by being boring.
Worked all my life and paid my share,
I need to be selfish now, to write and to share

To scribble and doodle to dream and to muse,
I long to express my creative views.
To write poems, jokes and a story or two,
If your time was fading, what would you do?

Chronicle your past, jot down what you've said,
Write final love letters, before you are dead?
Recall all the embraces and the wee smiling faces?
The journeys to work and exotic places?

Recall your bitter sweet childhood,
Filled with love, but little food,
Conjure stories for wee ones, so close to your heart,
Of pirates and princesses and baddies who fart?

Record laughter and love, all the moments of pleasure,
Comedy characters, superheroes and treasure,
So, with some vigour, that's what I must do,
Before all my sand makes its way through.

TWIRL

For years I'd watched the lifeboat launch
By volunteers with a six pack or paunch,
Rushing half-dressed through a narrow street
Not knowing what dangers, they would meet

Brave men and women, day and night
Luminously dressed, were a common sight
Locals moving to clear a path
A danger at sea, is not a laugh

For months I'd done my basic training
Through, wind, snow and coastal raining
I memorised nautical terms, with no mistakes
And got used to my hair looking like Medusa's snakes

The three boys before me couldn't work out the TWIRL,
The helmsman said "forget you're a girl,
It's the details that matter at sea and on land,
Small details are what'll get you into the band"

The band they referred to is an acceptance
That you'd always go the distance
That you'd have each other's back
All that sail out, should come back

I studied the boat crew, five stood out,
The ones who attended, when there was a shout.
I listened and watched all the things that they said,
At a lock-in at the pub a light bulb came on in my head.

My testing day arrived and all five were there,
With a hand-written banner, saying "C'mon Claire"
I passed my practical and my theory,
And got invited to the pub for a celebration party

As we all walked in, the five took a seat
Close to the open fire to warm their feet
Helmsman spoke up "Let's have a Twirl"
Which might sound sexist if you are a girl?

I found my voice for the first time in ages
Remembering the TWIRL in all of its stages
I ordered "Tonic Whisky Irish Rum Lager" and
all five shook my hand.
It's the small details that matter if you're joining the band.

FAVOURITE FOOD

The Death Row Diner, you don't have to pay
If they had beds, you'd move in today,
An All-day Breakfast, served after noon
With coffee cups, the size of the moon.

Donuts, pastries, biscuits, cakes,
All the things an angel makes,
Lots of things to have for Lunch,
Embracing the novel idea of Brunch

Afternoon tea with lots of steam,
Various scones, fresh jam and cream,
Dainty sandwiches cut in triangles,
This place really covers all the angles

For lunch, haggis, neeps and tatties,
Pakora, Tikka Masala, Fresh Chapatis,
Fish, Chips and mushy peas
Cauliflower, Macaroni, both with cheese

Steaks with all the trimmings,
Puds with lots of custard steaming
You're salivating I can tell,
The Diners at the junction between Heaven and Hell

HAIL MARY

The phone was answered on the first ring,
"My name is Mary, can I help with anything?"
The words were in my heart and head,
Saying them was causing me almighty dread

"Can you tell me your name?"
Was the cool, calm request
"Can you tell me you're alright?
I believe that talking is best"

I struggled to speak and stammered a reply,
"I'm going to end it; I'm going to die,
She's left me, I'm lonely, I just want my wife,
The best thing for me, is to take my own life"

"Tell me about your wife," was Mary's reply,
I struggled to speak as I wanted to cry,
"She was my world, my reason for living,
She was kind and patient, loving and giving"

Fast forward to now and the police lady sitting opposite me,
Put down her pen, saying "D'you fancy some tea?"
I politely declined and she walked out the door;
I thought of my statement and stared at the floor.

The door then opened and a woman came in,
She sat in a wheelchair, with a friendly grin,
"I thought I'd pop in, as talking about suicide's scary,
You might recognise my voice. "Hi, I'm Mary"

POISONOUS

To casual observers, they look like hags,
Carrying tormented souls in their carrier bags.
They traffic in pain, despair and misery,
And the next victim on their list just happens to be me.

I made the mistake of telling a friend,
"I hate my life, I wish it would end"
I'd rejected the chance of being glamorous
Choosing to infamous over famous.

My ego was as wide as the Clyde,
My sympathy as cold as the water inside.
My empathy level was on the floor,
When my beloved walked out the door.

Your neighbours grass isn't always green,
There's days he's gonna vent his spleen!
The hags are coming, I now see nine.
The soul they seek is clearly mine.

I'm surrounded by them on this ridge,
My options fight or cross the bridge,
Their poisonous fangs pierce my skin
Draining blood and the evil within

Floating high above me, I can see,
A smiling Angel, watching over me,
"You know, you can really put up a fight.
Are you waiting for a guiding light?"

"The Devil has his evil way,
Leeching on the vulnerable and those astray,
Do something now, do something good,
Or end up being, just old hags food."

DIRECTION

On Christmas Day, Bill shouted YES!
They'd bought him a brand new GPS!
One you can download a celebrity voice
He did a lap of honour, shouting "CHOICE!"

He flicked through the options,
And made some decisions,
As he was reading through the instructions,
He noticed a highlighted section.

INSTALL DEVICE ON XMAS DAY
TEST DRIVE DEVICE AT MIDDAY
So he installed it in his Austin Metro
At 11:59 he was ready to go.

The GPS voice sounded like his dad,
This was the best gift he'd ever had!
"Drive up the hill to Florence Street,
Turn left at the Butchers where you buy your meat."

It knew his routine! Bill was delighted.
Where next he wondered, getting excited,
Driving for him, was a bit of a stress,
The GPS would stop him making a mess.

His parents, always kind and giving,
Would help him move, to supported living,
"It's time you spread your wings,
And got to experience different things"

The GPS gave him more directions,
And interrupted his latest reflections
He travelled five miles outside town,
Passing a burger place with a clown.

"Drive down the valley to the river,
Stop at the Rose and Crown for dinner."
He parked up, securing every door
He was looking forward to driving some more!

He walked inside, to shouts of "SURPRISE"
He could hardly believe his eyes
His family stood by a Christmas tree
He counted them quick, there were twenty-three.

They asked how he was, he answered "Grand"
They knew he had a thing about shaking hands,
Bill's mum helped put his Xmas jumper on
She was just delighted to see her son.

He's embraced inclusion over seclusion,
But she was under no illusion,
She loved her son, with all her heart,
But Bill's journey today, was only the start.

WISH

Looking for Pisces

"Desiderio" was on the High Street,
Well known for something Italian to eat,
Run by Natalia and Giorgio her Papa,
Who originally came from the city of Pisa.

In a mirror Natalia, caught her reflection
And said to herself "Make up needs reapplication.
In a month, I'm gonna be thirty,
It's time to get all crafty and flirty."

She'd set her heart on a Pisces Man
Her perfect match, as a Cancerian.
But here she was, young and single
Close to Christmas, with no jingle.

She unlocked the doors at midday,
And mouthed what her Papa would say
"A delicious meal for free,
If you're in, by the time I count to 3"

Slowly counting "one and two and"
The door opened and she saw a hand
It was opening, to let a woman walk in
Who was glamorous, tall and thin.

The man followed, Natalia smiled,
Now that's what makes a woman wild
Broad shoulders, tall, with a narrow waist
Now, he was just to her taste.

"Do you have a table free?"
She suddenly felt weak at the knee,
What a looker, what a voice,
He'd suddenly become Natalia's choice.

Clearing her throat, she nodded "Yes."
Wiping her sweaty palms on her dress,
She offered a table, close to the bar
She didn't want to admire him, from afar.

The woman smiled, as he pulled out her chair,
The bitch did some flicking of the hair
Natalia, was jealous, her face was red
Imagining different ways, the bitch was dead.

"Monday has become an interesting day"
Was the what the text she sent would say,
Instead her thoughts were interrupted
By the woman, utterly disgusted.

"I'm leaving, if that's what you're going to eat!"
Within seconds, she was on her feet
She strode quickly to the door
Then like magic, she was no more.

Natalia swooped right in to chat,
Sadly, handsome wasn't having that
He said "I had no idea, she was a vegan,
She should have said, before we began."

He offered to pay £50 for the visit
But Natalia wouldn't take it.
Instead saying "Come back anytime,
It's not like you've committed a crime"

He said he would, and then he left
And Natalia was suddenly bereft.
She thought of him for the rest of the day,
Rude things, at least that's all I'll say.

Tuesday morning, Natalia woke up
Toast and coffee, just one cup.
She opened up, like she always did,

Her disappointment barely hid.

No midday hunk of beef,
Came in to soothe her lonely grief.
She took a break at half past two
Who strolls in? Well, you know who.

This time he's with an older lady
Twinset wearing, with hair quite grey
"He certainly picks them" to herself she mused.
"Pick me and I'll keep you quite amused."

Natalia tried to listen in,
Is eavesdropping, really a sin?
She heard him ask about baby lotion
And something about a "big commotion"
The lady in grey, said "Thank you, but no."
He stood up, as she set off to go.
Her heart fell, he looked so depressed
A fact which made her feel distressed.

He paid the bill without speaking,
All the while furiously texting.
When she came back with his change,
He was gone, which was strange.

On Wednesday he came in with a hippy
On Thursday again, with someone "nippy"
Fridays lunch date, was even worse
It was like he had a dating curse.

On Saturday he wasn't in
So that night, Natalia took to gin.
She watched a "romcom" on the telly
And demolished a tub of Ben & Jerr.

Sunday was the bombshell day
That's what Natalia's text would say
"He was pushing a baby in a pram!

I nearly choked on my scone and jam"

————————————

Women are a mystery,
Well, at least they are to me.
The guys oblivious to her being hurt
He's no idea she's tried to flirt.

His life's been busy, doing stuff.
He's no idea Natalia's in a huff.
Three weeks have passed, or more
Since he last walked through the restaurant door.

The fickle hands of fate,
Have led us to this latest date
He's gone for lunch on a whim,
Unaware, Natalia wants a word with him

He strolls into the restaurant,
Hungry, but not sure what he wants
The lunch time customers have gone
He thinks "I guess I'll dine alone."

Natalia offers him a seat
And asks him "what would you like to eat?"
"I fancy something different" is his reply
Then spots the anger in Natalia's eye.

"Have I offended you?" He politely says,
Hoping, it's not going to be one of those days
She sits opposite him, uninvited
Takes a deep breath and then gets started.

"I notice your dining alone today,
where are your dates, all busy?"
"Is the baby with your wife?
Whilst you have a great life."

He burst out laughing, which just made her mad
"D'you think it's funny being a Dad?"
She noticed a steely look in his eye
"I think you should listen" was his reply.

His face was stony, his voice firm and curt,
Her anger fled when she saw his hurt.
"You think you've a right, judging me,
When you've not got the whole story?"

She bit her lip, her face went red,
Comebacks raced inside her head.
"The baby belongs to my sister,
I've been interviewing a baby sitter."

"I haven't dated for over a year,
My sisters been ill, so I moved here,
The last 3 weeks have been about changing a nappy,
So I hope that makes you very happy?"

Natalia's mouth was suddenly dry
She could hardly breath and wanted to die
What have I done, what have I said,
Were questions running around in her head.

He stood up to leave and she started to cry
He passed her a napkin, her tears to dry.
"I'm sorry" he said "for speaking so loud,
You look like you need a drink, if that is allowed?"

Whilst shaking, Natalia gets to her feet
"I'll get you a drink; I'm having a whisky neat"
He asked for a glass of red wine.
And offered to pay, but she declined.

For ten minutes they sat, in silence.
She took a breath, "In my defence"
He stood up and walked out the door

She just stared at the floor.

The sound of the Grandfather clock
Was all she heard, tick-tock-tick-tock
The passing minutes seemed like hours
Each memory, becoming horrors.

She stood up, pacing to and fro
Wanting to leave, but with nowhere to go
She screamed and shouted "Why me!
All I wanted was a perfect Pisces"

"Well, I think you need to know
That's not happening, I'm a Virgo"
She turned to see him at the door
Her legs gave way, she hit the floor

He helped her up, into a chair
For the first time, noticing her lovely hair
He wiped the tears from her eyes
Which were green, to his surprise.

He's Pleasant, Interesting, Sympathetic, Charm-
ing Empathetic and Single.
"Do you fancy a date, a Christmas Jingle?"

ΩA

Zeus stamped his foot upon the floor
"Young ones are dying by the score,
Xanadu is what we agreed,
When was love replaced with greed?"

Venus mumbled, shedding tears
"Universally, Earth is the worst I fear,
The other planets are trouble free
Some humans break the heart in me."

Rhadamanthys, speaking for the mortals
Questioned, all the other immortals
"Possibly, we need another war
Or bring Poseidon to their shore?"

Neptune stood up to say,
"Make them unify, behind a tragedy
Let's resonate a clarion chord
Kindness must be restored"

Jupiter, the god of thunder and sky
Intervened "I'm just the guy,
Hailstorms, lighting, hurricane
Global warming is already insane"

Fate was sealed upon that day
Earth was finally, going to pay
Desperate times, were to be had
Countless people would be sad

But, the Gods decision can be converted
Armageddon can be averted

BLETHER

I don't often sigh.

Today I sighed .

In fact, I sighed a lot

One sigh started in my socks and worked its way up to being a MEGA sigh.

The sighs started when I realised that I'd forgotten to charge my mobile.

My phone charger was in the living room connected to my iPad.

My phone angel; the ever helpful spare battery that always gives me an "hour of power", was probably in the bowl on the coffee table or lost, again.

I continued sighing more deeply when it dawned on me that I'd forgotten to bring my earphones for my mobile phone.

I can't even put them in and pretend I'm listening to something and filter out the noise and chatter that's enveloping me on the bus.

I genuinely feel like the Court of Human Rights has let me down.

My civil liberties are being infringed by SPT.

I know they're called Strathclyde Partnership for Transport but it's like they've said "OK, let's make this journey a combination of torpor and torture."

Yep. Strathclyde Partnership for Torture. That's going to be their name when I'm elected President of Scotland. "Taking the bus" is now the modern day equivalent of the stocks, that was as popular as a punishment in the 16th and 17th Century.

Take today for instance.

The wee man behind me on the bus is making noises that David Attenborough hasn't heard. I think he's trying to cough out his pancreas.

There are two wee women in front of me that I'm going to politely refer to as the Witches of Wishaw.

I've placed my sports bag and coat on the vacant seat beside me, it's the window seat. I've done this, in an obvious attempt to discourage anyone sitting beside me and negatively impacting on me physically, mentally, emotionally, spiritually or holistically.

The mean spirited, horrendously hatted harridan in front of me is called Elsie and her pal is a dreary dragon in the pink Pacamac, is Betty. Nobody living or dying in their street are not getting discussed, dissected, defamed, shamed and blamed. Elsie the British Bulldog is ranting on about how Brexit's impacting on the price of her Co-op Croissants and Camembert.

Her rough voice could remove rust off a bridge.

Betty has just adjusted her hat for the twentieth time in the last two minutes and swore "As long as I live I'll never shop in that Ladles or Alldays" pointing to the two German supermarkets, that are on either side of the road into Glasgow.

Betty occasionally communicates without swearing and has obviously been a deep sea diver in the past as she's got the ability to speak without taking a breath for upwards of four minutes

It's starting to rain, in fact it's pouring down

As the bus has slowly but inevitably filled up I have no choice but to move to the window seat as a damp, fleece-wearing lady reeking of lavender sits beside me and asks "Where are you going?" and "Is that you off to work?"

I silently shake and nod my head to avoid having to breathe in the ladies toxic fumes. Smiling is not an option as I value the enamel on my teeth

The coffin dodger behind me, now appears to have both eyes in one socket due to his coughing fits turning into apoplectic seizures. If you were to take an old man and soak him in Vimto for a month you'd not get the purple he was now displaying.

As the purple man gets up to leave the bus, two young lads in football tops of famous Spanish sides proceed to discuss the game from the night before.

Names like Messi, Bale, Ramos and Suarez, fly back and forth between them in a broad Scottish accent but with a subtle attempt at Spanish. They overemphasise the word "Barcelona" about a dozen times, laughing at each other's attempts

Betty and Elsie have arrived at their stop, beside the Bingo Hall. They take their time leaving the bus to say "Hi and Goodbye" to everyone and that includes the driver.

I dread the thought of them both jumping back on again to pick up a Metro and consider it an encore.

The seats are taken up by two old guys who are debating Brexit. David Cameron, the former prime minister is being defended by the gravelly voiced baldy guy with the Barbour jacket.The other guy is on the attack and has a posh Morningside accent. Both of them agree that Westminster should be levelled to the ground or made into student accommodation.

I'm now trying to breathe through one nostril as the essence of lavender is like a chloroform cloak. I unzip my bag and pretend to look inside whilst breathing in reasonably fresh air that's contained within.

At the second stop after the Bingo, an inspector checks all our tickets and lets us know that there's a diversion. Everyone from the council to pot holes via marches of various religions is blamed for the delay. As we pass by the diversion signs we note roadworks that leads to opinions on gas, electric and various cable companies.

The additional ten minutes on the bus reminded me of why we have banned torture in Scotland. If you don't believe me, try not breathing without needing to go to the toilet.

My stop is coming up and as I step off the bus, I see my supervisor outside the building having a vape.

"I tried calling you, but your phones switched off" he says matter of factly. He continues "We've had a power cut, something to do with local roadworks, we've sent all non-essential staff home, so I'll see you tomorrow."

The MEGA sigh begins. The screaming inside my head is like a plane taking off,

As the rain hammers down, I turn and head for the bus home.

METAL

I was a soldier in a war,
Sadly, I'm not involved anymore.
One unlucky day, my judgment was poor,
I stood on a landmine, beneath a floor.

That's when I briefly learnt to fly,
It's OK. If I don't laugh, I'll cry,
Metal shrapnel, designed to kill,
Certainly, put me through the mill

Battle Casualty! First Aid!
Was the first response, they made,
Using a camouflage scarf and knife,
A tourniquet was made, to save my life .

Colleagues, thought, I'd soon be dead,
I see, Helicopter rotors overhead.
Casualty evacuating me instead.
I woke - days later - in a bed .

Metal machines were everywhere,
Totally bald, they'd shaved my hair.
Metal needles, were in my skin,
Sat crying, was my next of kin .

A Hercules transport plane,
Had brought me home again
As drugs wore off, I felt the pain,
I thought that I would go insane

———

The bad bit now, so here we go,
I've spent 6 months in physio,
It's really not been good for me,
Accepting no legs, below the knee

We joke amongst us, in the military,
Because we are as close as family,
We don't say, "how'd you lose them?"
Because, I know where I left 'em.

So I've gone from strengthening a Corp
To physically, strengthening my core.
They keep yelling "More, more, more"
It's for my benefit, I know the score.

Find a job, a home, a partner,
Attempting, a "Happy ever after"
Life's a challenge for us all,
I wish the Government was on the ball.

They were quick enough to get me there,
I can't complain about my medical care,
But now I'm back, I am deflated,
About how low, rehabilitations rated.

We live in a civilised society,
I'm not complaining, just for me,
Politicians aren't shy in spending wealth,
Just spend some, on our mental health.

It's not just me, with PTSD
Take a look around and see,
Police Officers and Emergency Crew,
Fire Fighters, to name a few.

The problem for me,
Is not, my so called disability,
It's how I'm viewed, by strangers,
They feel compelled to highlight dangers.

I genuinely, have no doubt,
Government, will pull their finger out,

But indeed it has to be said,
"Can you do it, before I'm dead?"

So it's metal legs for me,
I'm footloose and fancy free,
It's my chat up line, a joke,
As I'm still a single bloke

But I have a cunning plan,
For the Paralympics in Japan,
Be it Bronze, Silver or even Gold,
I plan to get some metal to hold.

If I get selected, for Invictus,
That would be, a major plus
But, at least I'm in the game,
Pride, is slowly replacing shame.

Wish me luck, wish me well,
I might just win, only time will tell,
But, I will never admit defeat,
One day, I'll stand on my own 2 feet.

HOPE

The feckless, travel from near and far,
By train, plane and even car,
They've left at home, their heart and pride,
Ambition, their rollercoaster ride.

They hold their noses, as they pass,
The homeless lad, the jobless lass
With jaundiced eye they view,
The public that is me and you

Deep in their chambers of power,
They gather like a monsoon shower,
Miserable, drab and soaking wet,
Is this the best leadership, we can get ?

As slippery as the slipperiest soap
Our politicians, handle our hope.
It's privilege and profit, profile and power
That consumes their every hour

The NHS, I must confess,
Is sadly, a bureaucratic mess,
Consumed by mountains of paperwork
Hire a nurse, not a clerk!

High speed trains, crime in each city,
The exorbitant cost of university
Terrorism and immigration,
The economy is in stagnation

Homeless veterans in the street,
Children starving, nothing to eat
Pensioners can't afford their heat
Or to watch TV as a treat.

Knife crime murders nearly every day,
I believe an uprising is on the way
There's prospect of no medicine or food
Not sure a general election, is any good

We are now, a divided society,
Millions with nothing and a few who party,
The thieves who sold us PPI
The banks who failed us, so I ask why?

Why are we so resistant
To voicing our intent
To get back our treasured country
For the grandchildren, of you and me

We vote them in, so vote them out,
Rally, March, Petition, Shout,
Don't dilly dally or delay,
They're washing your hope's away

Our future, should be in our hands,
Not influenced, by Euros, Dollars, Rands,
Or by those who wish to profit,
From the misery that is Brexit.

VIBRATION

It was Daphne's first Ann Summers party,
Some of the mums, looked a bit tarty,
She had some nibbles, a little wine,
Everything seemed to be just fine

Various items caught her eye,
Things for a woman, things for her guy
She had more drink, than necessary,
She was carried home by her pal, Mary

She woke to find a bag of stuff,
Regretting that she felt so rough,
Some coffee and paracetamol,
Helped her gain back some control

A five o'clock she answered the door
To seven smiling neighbours
They all piled in, "we love your house"
Daphne was stunned, as quiet as a mouse

"You invited us for cocktails, today"
Was all the girls would say
Two hours later and smashed again,
No more hangover, no more pain

Her husband Edward, in from work
Is stunned, perplexed, he cannot talk
There's drunken women everywhere,
Wolf whistling him, without a care.

Daphne, in one hand has a drink,
And in the other, something very pink
Daphne giggles "This is a great invention,
It makes fabulous cocktails, by its vibration".

EMOTION

Those who really know me believe,
I wear my heart upon my sleeve,
I don't pretend somethings in my eye,
I'm a guy, of course I cry

That moment, before an oration,
Or an unexpected, standing ovation,
Your response to adulation
A false voice, saying "Congratulations"

When your team, scores a winning goal,
A child's been rescued from a hole,
Hearing the National Anthem play,
Or Last Post on Remembrance Day

When you put up the Christmas tree,
That moment of going from I to We,
Marriage vows and wedding rings,
And all the joy that family brings

Some humorous mirth,
Your children's birth,
A loved one's death,
Moments, when you lose your breath

A stomach, that has a butterfly,
You wonder why, your mouth's so dry?
Emotions, taking over you,
You've been there, you know it's true

That farewell kiss,
The one you miss
A babies cry,
Bring emotions, I won't deny.

MAP

Gloria's SATNAV was broken
For an hour it hadn't spoken,
She phoned her dad to ask for help,
The alternative, was to look up YELP

"There's a road map in the glove compartment"
He said, providing a useful hint,
She stared at all the various pages,
This would take her, bloody ages

She called the AA without any luck,
Considered using a pick up truck,
An hour passed, somehow she survived,
Until her lovely Dad arrived

With mum, who wasn't smiling.
Not like Dad, who was willing,
To help her in her emergency,
That was now a full on tragedy

Mum drove away their car,
Dad took me in mine, it wasn't far,
He muttered "You know, you have 2 legs,
It would have been quicker to walk to Greggs"

SUCTION

I really don't know,
If, in Guantanamo,
They've made a decision,
To use as torture, suction,

I bring this to your attention,
As I really need to mention,
An experience, from my youth,
And I'll try not to be, uncouth

I was still in my teens,
Trying to look trendy in jeans,
Out drinking with a friend,
When my life was about to end.

A drunken female accosted me,
When I'd had a beer or three,
Not many women, in the human race,
Have tried to kiss, my innocent face.

She was an assaulter, not a smoother,
Attacking me, like a human hoover,
She lip locked me, with a suction,
That had a very strange reaction

I couldn't breathe, my legs gave way,
I still get nightmares, till this day,
I felt powerless, below my hips,
I recall the taste of Gin and chips,

Her tongue was huge, I needed air,
But she tightly gripped me, by my hair,
The room was full of people laughing,
And my head was really spinning.

I tried to be a gentleman,
And ease her off, as best I can,
I knew touching her, would be risky,
In case she thinks I'm getting frisky.

She applies more power to the kiss,
I roll my eyes, she thinks its bliss,
The suction increases, even more,
I wake up later, on the floor

The barmaid's looking down on me,
With a mixture of concern and pity
"Now you've finished, with romancing,
She wants, to take you to the dancing"

So if you want terrorists to admit,
The targets that they plan to hit,
And want to save property and life
I know a torturer, she's my mates wife.

MULTIPLY

Davie, took the witness stand,
Held the bible in his hand,
Even though he only had one tooth,
He promised he would tell the truth

"As you all can plainly see,
I have no teeth to lie through to thee"
Davie was a holy man,
But loved a lager from a can

The judge knew Davie, very well,
He was always in a Police cell,
"Tell us what happened on Friday Night"
Whispering "Let's have no shite"

Davie was a storyteller,
Described by many, as an OK fella,
Liked a drink, was often loud,
Liked being centre of attention, to a crowd

"I'd been having a small libation,
In the alley behind the station,
Two cops turned up on a bike,
One called Andy, the other Mike"

Shaking the wig on his head,
The judge wearily said,
"Davie, I think it's really best
That you get to the bit, about your arrest

Davie shrugged and carried on,
"I was only joking, having fun,
I didn't say F*** Off, that's a lie,
I said, why don't go off and Multiply"

The courtroom, laughed out loud
Davie puffed his chest out proud,
The judge, did not look happy,
Banging his gavel, very snappy

"The judgment of this court,
Based on what you said and thought,
Is usually a fine of 40 or 50,
But I'll make it 200, as I like to Multiply."

SPRAY

The colour chart was off the scale,
Too many choices for a Male,
My beloved, spoke "I think it's good,
To have something like redwood.

The assistant said, "I've got to say,
The most popular colour, is mahogany"
They looked at charts for ages,
Whilst flicking through catalogue pages.

A young girl offered coffee or tea,
And soon a cup was brought to me,
I loudly coughed "My opinion as a man,
Is, I want this coffee colour, for my spray tan"

THE FINAL SLEEP

Before I take my final sleep,
I have things to say, I'm going deep,
My nightmares, secrets, I shall keep
This final journey's been too steep.

I really miss the army welfare,
Someone, who would dare to care,
A sanctuary, for us all to share,
Treated, firm, friendly, but fair.

I was taught well, to obey,
So, I packed my stuff away,
There's not much more to say,
I just can't face another day,

I have a cap badge in my pocket,
In the other, there's a locket,
I feel a pain in my eye socket,
But I die tonight, so fuck it.

I don't want to recall,
Or recoil, to the horror of it all,
So, as I lie, against a piss stained wall
I can hear, Big Ben's midnight call

I'm calmer now, I've taken medication,
Enough to go beyond sedation,
I do not want your resuscitation,
If possible, I'd like a Viking cremation?

Now, my heart will only allow
My breathing, to be very shallow
With a kerb, as my concrete pillow
I embrace the glow, it's time to go

So if you find me in the street,
I'm sorry, this is how we meet
Think of me as smart and tough,
Who admitted "enough's enough"

I reminisce, of far flung places,
Of fallen comrades, with smiling faces
Different colours, creeds and races
And with my final breath, I say my Graces.

DISTRACTION

I got a call "Can you help me?
I need picking up from the A&E"
It wasn't late, he is a mate,
I had nothing else, on my plate

The waiting room was packed,
Some on mobiles, whilst others snacked,
Eventually, he appeared,
He looked worse, than I had feared.

Bandaged head, leg in plaster,
I couldn't hold in, my laughter,
"What happened mate?" I enquired
And noticed that his jaw was wired

Through gritted teeth, he told a story,
It was grim and gritty, very gory,
He'd been at a party and got attracted,
to a Femme Fatale and got distracted,

I asked him, "Were you full of beer,
Doing daft dancing, again on a chair?"
He shook his head to answer No.
He explained himself, whispering slow

"A schoolboy error, I performed,
Again, I wasn't fully informed,
This is the worst day of my life,
I tried to chat up, a pal of my wife"

"The wife, stormed into the room,
Like a Whizzy Witch on a broom,
She punched and kicked me everywhere
I'm lucky that I've still got hair"

"My bodies, Black and Blue,
I'm walking like I've had a poo,
My genitalia is swollen by two,
Can I stay the night with you?"

So it's taxi time for us,
There's no way he'll survive the bus
So the moral of this fiction,
Is Distraction, can lead to friction.

FRIENDSHIP

You're feeling isolated,
depressed, deflated
Browbeaten, into submission,
In a state of anger and frustration.

You've nowhere to go or hide,
No matter how hard you've tried,
A river of tears, have been cried,
Suddenly, a friend is by your side

They'll help, without judging you,
Because they know, that's what you would do,
Those on your side, through hardship
Are in your golden circle of friendship

You won't let many, get close enough,
As most, can't handle the messy stuff,
I don't mean those who'll dry your tears,
And listen to you, over some beers

I mean the ones who really listen,
Who know, that bullshit doesn't glisten
By giving advice, that's good and smart,
They can help rebuild, a broken heart

They may not live close by,
You might not speak every day,
But when the shit, has hit the fan
They're the ones who Do and Can

We don't enjoy many in our life,
Who'll take on our troubles and strife,
Embrace, their love and kindness
Because, they are - truly - priceless.

HIDDEN

The secret, can't be shared,
No one must know, you cared,
That glimpse, that furtive look,
The mission you undertook

Checking, that you've not been seen,
Not confirming, where you've been,
Taking on the persona of a spy,
Avoiding conversations, with "Hi"
and "Bye"

Secretly hiding everything,
Paper, bow, sparkling string,
Locked away in your locker,
At the hospital, where you're a worker

You hope her pulse will race,
Put a smile upon her face,
And a sparkle in her eyes,
Will it come as a surprise?

Nearly a month has past,
The big day's arrived at last.
It's hidden well, deep in the tree,
The Secret Santa gift, from me.

CREEP

The doubt, began to creep,
Just before, I fell asleep,
Once again, I got out of bed,
It has crept into my head,

I go downstairs, check the alarm,
Yes it's on, I'm feeling calm,
Fridge and freezer, doors secure,
I check them twice, to be sure

Electrical goods switched off,
Then I unplug them, with a huff,
Kettle, TV, coffee grinder,
Her hairdryer and curler/roller

Washing machine, tumble dryer,
And that never used, deep fat fryer,
Windows and doors are all fine,
The cork is in the bottle of wine

Go back to bed, snuggle up tight
I jump out of bed, something's not right
I quietly curse the thing that I did miss,
And I let the dog out for a piss.

SUSPICIOUS

Belle and Billy, quietly ate their food,
It was their 4th visit, it was very good
As usual Billy offered to pay,
They'd always argue, it was their way.

They'd been separately hired as a PI
Yep, Private Investigators eating pie,
You couldn't make it up, if you tried
A budding romance, couldn't be denied

The targets, AKA the Principals
Clearly, had no principles,
He was more handy, than a squid
She ate 'n drank, without paying a quid

Arriving separately at a Wetherspoons
Every Tuesday in the afternoons,
Huddled, whispering, never a shout,
It was more a Steak In, than a Stakeout

As the couple were acting mysterious,
It made the PI's very suspicious,
They covertly photographed the pair,
Who to be fair, didn't seem to care.

Belle and Billy stepped outside,
To Vape and quietly confide,
The couple joined them for a fag,
And overheard the woman nag.

"You've got to grow yourself a pair,
Tell her, that you no longer care"
The guy looked at his shuffling feet,
Taking his bollocking in the street.

He mumbled back "You're all the same
How come, I am the one to blame"
he slapped him hard upon his head,
"By the way, you're shite in bed"

Belle and Billy, held in laughter,
Trying to work out who's the dafter
They silently giggled, with tears in eyes,
As the love affair, came to a demise

"Let's say, we have nothing to report,
I think a rude lesson has been taught"
Belle agreed with Billy's observation,
"To be fair, I didn't get the fascination"

That night, they went their separate ways,
Submitted reports, within two days,
The hiring partners, seemed relieved,
That they had not been deceived

Belle and Billy lived separate lives,
No romance here, as both have wives,
This story has a happy ending,
But then again, I'm just pretending.

SHALLOW

I've dug a grave,
it's very shallow,
I've got no choice,
Beneath mines, another fellow.

I'm burying a bad guy,
Not a gangster or a spy,
Just an average Joe
Who really had to go

No fond farewell, no oratory,
No recognition in a cemetery,
No flowers or a card,
Missing him, will be hard.

A man known by the local police,
For lots of things, including vice.
Not known for buying anyone a beer,
News of his death, would raise a cheer

The only ones, that will look,
Are those searching for his debtors book,
The book's now burning, in my fire,
As promised, when I took the hire

My daily rates are not negotiable,
Killing children's, off the table,
My legitimate job, a magician's act,
I make things disappear, that's a fact.

YOUR HEART

We all, have a very complex Heart,
With a bit of love in every part,
Every particle, in each ventricle,
Dedicated, to different people.

But, do we really get to choose,
Whom, to keep or who to lose?
Broken pieces, from your past,
May remain, or never last.

How do we decide who stays inside?
When Giving your heart is implied,
Is it measured, by tears you've cried
Or how many times, you've tried.

Lover, artist, writer, singer,
We all put it, through the wringer,
It's a muscle, made of sturdy stuff,
What doesn't kill us, makes us tough

Your heart, helps you laugh and cheer
Forms a smile from ear to ear,
Bring lumps to throats, creates a tear,
Is ever present, in sadness and fear

Without one, we can not survive,
It's the thing that keeps us alive,
Quite often, we give it to another,
Some cherish the gift, some don't bother

In those moments, it feels like grief,
The solitude, a pain beyond belief
That gut wrenching, screaming pain,
"Never again" says, your brain

Each piece of heart, carefully collected
Is stored, awaiting, to be reconstructed,
Bits remain missing, lost forever,
Years go by and you become wiser.

I love my Heart, that keeps me warm,
That does it's best, to keep me calm,
Has led me into safety and harm,
Encouraging, love, kindness and charm.

When your sand runs through,
Consider asking "What should I do?
Is it worth the bother?
Donating it to another?"

Is it, the gift of life?
Can it take more love or strife?
Is it up for another, rollercoaster ride?
Well, I guess, only you can decide.

GUEST WRITERS

Dice - Shane Noone

The Wanderer - Shane Noone

Gorbals Writing Group

The Covenant - Sam McGurran

Gandhi Ashram, India - Nikita Gurav

The Murder - Nikita Gurav

Wee Blether - Marjorie A.M. Ferry

Kick In The Creatives

WHAT???!!! - Ellen Kerr

Johnny Delaney - Sheryll Martin

Lucky Girl Am I - Sheryll Martin

In Search of Faerie Nuff

Lucky Star - Lucy A Levason

DICE

By Shane Noone

Rolled. In need of luck.
Many faces. Many sides.
Thrown away. Picked up.
A lost mans cause.
A gamblers investment.
Win a drink
Win a job!?
Work isn't cutting it. Taking you nowhere.
In need of a break.
But are you ready?
Rolling through life.
From table to table.
Owner's hand to owner's hand.
Everyone's grubby prints leaving their mark.
When did you take this form?
Become this object?
You were the hand.
You were meant to be the one deciding.
A moment of ambition.
Has turned you into ...
This item of vice
This tumbling dice

THE WANDERER

By Shane Noone

You reach a point
Like the wanderer through the wastelands
The mad lands
The Bad lands

The wanderer has done things to survive
Done mad things
Done bad things

This is a dark land. A solo, lonely journey.
Parts of the land are scorched.
Burned.

You will get no sustenance or comfort in these parts again
For it was you who burned them
Like fire, who's greed eats up all the air around it
Your greed ate up all the good and has left waste
Scars

Like the scars that cover you,
Scars you received early on your journey,
Have sent you this direction
Have sent you through this barren land
And caused you to destroy those places of comfort along the way
For fear they beat you to it and catch fire while you sleep
and fall down around you

With thick, dark smoke choking and suffocating you
Rendering you useless to defend against the fire that kisses
against your new skin
Your hardened scar tissue

After a long time on this journey After stopping at many towns
along the way

Where the wanderer enjoyed wild debauched stays
For moments of respite and flashes of what passed for happiness
The wanderer reaches a point on their journey
Where they meet a high wall

This place seems new to them
Not like before
The wanderer doesn't know for sure
But senses there may be something good in this town

Flashes of clear skies and daylight flicker through cracks in the
wall
And softly touch our wanderer
Filling body, mind and soul with warmth
Tingling from a feeling rare and alien on this journey

In this town the dark, red, grey clouds don't blanket the sky
Here there is the possibility of more

You didn't expect to find this place
You chose this direction to run away from such places
For such places made you soft and weak
And in travelling through this apocalyptic wasteland you know
you need to be tough to survive
And you have become an expert in this type of survival

But now, time or cold, or the thrill of something new
Has you reach your hand out to that slice of light
Like a flashlight beam shining a path through dusk

It beams onto your hand
And the warmth fills you
Like liquid fills a hollow shape

You close your eyes. Keep your arm outstretched
And for a moment, you get lost in dreams of how
wonderful more of this could be.

Covenant - Sam McGurran

Gandhi Ashram, India - Nikita Gurav

The Murder - Nikita Gurav

A Wee Blether - Marjorie A.M. Ferry

COVENANT

By Sam McGurran

The desert was an unforgiving place. Everything that lived here was yoked to two great threats; thirst and exposure. Konrad feared both.

It was an hour before dawn and already the desert was beginning to warm. He ran as fast as he could, even considering abandoning his precious armour. He considered giving up too; allowing himself to be cooked alive.

Then he saw the cave. It was still some distance away, but he could see clearly the darker shadow amidst the shades of the fading night.

He had almost made it to the mouth of the cave when he smelled blood. He halted, breathing deeply. There was no mistaking the coppery tang. He knew he was leagues from the nearest crusader camp, which could only mean one thing: Saracen. Caught between an

injured foe and the rising sun, Konrad knew what he had to do. He stepped into the cave, sword drawn and held out his waterskin. The cave was dark, despite the growing light outside, but Konrad could make out a figure propped up against the far wall. He saw a reddish smudge on the wall beside him. "You're hurt," he said. Easing further into the cave, avoiding the first rays of dawn, he settled onto his haunches, putting up his sword. He saw something in the man's hands and smelt the oil of the mechanism. A crossbow. "A *ferengi* in the hands of a Saracen?" he asked, in flawless Arabic. The man shifted slightly and Konrad could see there was a bolt loaded into the groove.

"We do what we must," said the man.

His voice was deep and gruff, but Konrad thought he detected a note of pain. He laid his sword on the ground beside him.

"You must go."

Konrad glanced out at the ever-growing brightness and shook his head. "I can't do that."

The tip of the crossbow raised ever so slightly, pointing at Konrad's chest. At this range, even a standard bolt would punch through his armour like cloth and skewer his heart.

"Easy. We don't have to be enemies," Konrad, offered the waterskin again, "Are you thirsty?"

The man's aim never wavered. "You would offer water to a dying Saracen?"

Konrad shrugged. "I'd offer water to a thirsty man."

The Saracen looked at him and nodded, as if to himself. "I will take your water. Throw it to me."

Konrad cocked his head, "Take your finger from the trigger. I don't want to be shot if you fumble the catch."

"I will be careful."

Konrad tossed him the water. As predicted, the man failed to catch the skin. His other arm barely twitched though, keeping the crossbow steady. As his hand scrambled around in the dust for the water, his eyes never moved from Konrad. Konrad himself settled back, forcing himself to relax. Thirst burned at his throat and his teeth ached, but he wouldn't show it.

The Saracen's fingers closed around the waterskin and he raised it to his lips; pulling free the cork with his teeth. He sipped carefully, swirling the precious liquid around his mouth. When he had finished he sealed it again with his chin, unwilling to lay down his weapon for even a second. "Thank you," he said, tossing the skin back.

It fell a little short, but Konrad leant forward and plucked it out of the air with ease. He reattached it to his belt. "Tell me, why haven't you shot me?"

"You want me to shoot you?" The Saracen cocked his head.

Konrad chuckled, getting as comfortable as he could against the hard rock. "No. By your own admission you are dying, so in your final hours surely you would want to take more of the infidel with you? Or show mercy and put aside your weapon. Yet you have done neither," Konrad studied the dark face, it was clear now. His caramel skin was framed by charcoal coloured hair and beard. His moustache looked like it had been well groomed, but now it held the dust and dirt of the desert, as did the rest of him. An ugly brand, in the shape of a crescent moon, was burned into his cheek. *Recently*, Konrad thought.

The Saracen let out a slow breath. "I do not know what Allah wishes me to do. You Frankish demons are a plague upon the Holy Land," he gestured with the crossbow.

Konrad grinned despite himself.

The Saracen gently touched the brand on his cheek. "Yet…it was not the Franks who left me to die." After a moment he lowered the crossbow, till it pointed at Konrad's feet.

Konrad sat up a little straighter. "If Allah is anything like Christ, he is not clear on what he wants." It was a mistake. The crossbow point swung up again.

"You dare blaspheme?" hissed the Saracen.

Konrad sat forward and locked eyes with the man.

"I do. Has not your god left you to die? The Holy Land… Ha. All gods have forsaken Outremer. Christian, Hebrew or Saracen, we are not so different. All are misled by loud men and false gods. Not I." Konrad got slowly to his feet.

"Then your soul is damned!" snarled the Saracen.

"Yes, I rather think it is," said Konrad. He took a step towards the Saracen, who aimed the crossbow at his heart.

"No further demon." Konrad grinned again, taking another step.

"You think by suffering an agonising death, your god will notice? What is your name Saracen?"

The man looked troubled. "Suleiman."

Konrad took another step. "Suleiman. I can take the pain away. Would you like that?"

They stared at each other, the fallen Saracen and the tall knight. Suleiman could see now the knight's white tabard was stained with crimson and his armour bore none of the crucifixes and religious icons that were common among Crusaders.

"I…do not wish to die," said Suleiman.

Konrad's face was still in shadow but there was a light in his eyes.

"And you won't," he murmured, bending over Suleiman, "but you will never see another sunrise."

Suleiman fired.

Konrad hissed and staggered back, staring down at the wooden shaft protruding from his stomach. Then he sighed.

"You missed."

Reaching down, he slowly pulled the bolt from his body, throwing it out into the sunlight where it sizzled and spat.

Suleiman watched in wide-eyed horror.

Konrad stooped again, grabbing Suleiman's wrist in an iron grip, making him drop his dagger. "I like you, Suleiman, I really do. You're a thinker. But I... I'm thirsty."

Konrad's eyes blazed like hot coals and Suleiman screamed. Konrad bit into his throat and at last; he drank.

Konrad watched as the sunlight slowly retreated towards the mouth of the cave. He couldn't see the sun, but knew it was sinking towards the horizon as the minutes passed. At last, he looked out on the grey sand and sighed.

"Vampires in a desert." He shook his head. "I want to see trees again, rivers too. Venice. Paris. Rome. I feel ready for a change, what about you?"

Suleiman stepped up beside him. He was tall and broad-shouldered, his torn clothes stained with his own blood. His skin looked paler, but his eyes burned.

"I feel... thirsty."

GANDHI ASHRAM, INDIA

By Nikita Gurav

I implore you to look at it with deep thought.

Look at it brick by brick,

Let the white, rough, mortarish lines guide your eyes,

Slowly creeping up towards those grey projecting brackets,

That grey mass of horizontal expanse bind-
ing the structure together,

Guiding yet allowing freedom to explore those
volumes of light and shade,

Volumes of rough and smooth,

and of white and blue.

A space within a space, nestled together with openness.

Tying your eyes down to the ground with Trans-
parent thought and feeling....

THE MURDER

By Nikita Gurav

Step by step I walked on the rusty roads of life.
Made every move thoughtfully and courageously.
My head only bent bent down in thought but
never once in shame.
I always held my head high with pride and honour,
but, what is this that I stand upon today?
Something so terrible and so shocking!
How could I do it ? How could I do such a hideous thing
It is with these very hands that I did it,
These hands were once looked upon as hard workers,
But, today they have proved themselves to be murderers!

Ohh what should I do now? I have lost something very precious,
Its presence in my life has been priceless.
Let me tell you friends, it is not a person that I speak of here,
It is faith that I killed! I have lost faith in myself.
I have killed it with my very own hands.

When one loses faith in oneself, it's like having wings without any feathers,
It's like trying to chop wood with a blunt axe and
like fishing without a fishing rod.
It was faith that instilled life in me, every-
time I thought I had lost.
It was faith alone that stood by me when no one held my hand,
It was faith alone that shone brightly like the
sun, when there was no light.

I have lost my greatest asset today,
and yes! It's me who is the culprit.
How could I let just one defect wash it all away?
Wash it away forever and ever!

I have been defeated before but this defeat is the greatest.
It is the greatest because the loss is the greatest.

I know not what to do.
I know not what to say
But only that I am helpless without my faith.
I will surely live because I can still breathe
But , I will also not live because I have no faith in me.

A WEE BLETHER

By Marjorie A.M. Ferry

'That's my Soap starting', Annie would say. 'Away you down the pub Archie and get a wee blether. See who's in'.

I've been coming to The Loch Inn – or the lock-up as the punters call it, it's no very big - for nearly 20 years. Seen it change hands manies the time. It was always the same story. Quiet. Hard to get the punters in. It's a busy place on weekends but folk can't really afford a wee night out mid-week anymore. I'd sit at my usual table in the corner, drinking my stout, staring into space, just as contented as Nell, the pub's collie dog sitting by my feet

An odd time, the door would open and a few young guys spill in. That would start up a wee bit of life in the place. Stacey the barmaid always has a wee laugh with them. The talk was always football. Everybody had an opinion, everyone making sure they got their tuppence-worth in. 'See what I would do if I was that manager'.

This night the doors burst open and about fifteen or more of them pile in. All in high spirits. Really livened up the place. Stacey turned the music up to audible levels. Next thing I know she comes over with a pint. 'The guys sent that over Archie'.

'Hello Grandad, do you want a wee shot?', the youngest looking one says.

'Och no, that would probably kill me', I says.

Next thing I know he's back with a dark rum. Obviously asked Stacey what my tipple was. That fair warmed me up from the inside out.

'It's Kyle's stag do', he says to me. What's your name?', and before

I could answer the doors were flung open again and the cheers went up. They'd got him a strip-o-gram. The lassie was awfy bonny. She did a wee turn, great singer, smashing voice and what a dancer. She took it all off down to red tassels and wee red heart panties.

As is usual nowadays it was all selfies, then Kyle, the groom, brings her over and they take a selfie with me. I was smiling ear to ear. 'Wait 'til I tell Annie all about this'. And then the boys were away, off on the next leg of the stag.

'Do you mind if I join you while I'm waiting on my lift Archie?', Patricia asks. Fully dressed by now, you understand.

I was delighted by the company. She tells me about how she got into the strip-o-gram lark, she's an actress, and often between jobs. Good money for a wee half hour gig', she says, 'and the tips are great'.

She also does a Ghost Walk and a Rennie Mackintosh tour, stuff like that. I says, 'Patricia I never knew there was such a thing. My Annie loves Rennie Mackintosh.'

Then she tells me that she usually has a minder with her when she does stags and parties. 'You never really know what you're stepping into Archie. Very seldom get any bother, but it's good for punters to see a minder, keeps them in check. But my minder, he's moved up to Fife, met a woman on-line. You wouldn't be interested Archie, would you?', she asked me. Well, I was taken aback.

'I'm maybe a bit auld for that Patricia', I says .

'You only need to go into the venue ahead of me, give the staff the name of the person who's booked me, then get him to identify the recipient. Come and get me and I do all the rest. You'd really be helping me out'.

And before I know it Annie's insisting I wear my best suit; I say no to those new uncomfortable shoes she bought me for Alex's funeral though.

'I might be standing about a bit Annie; I want to be comfortable'.

And that's how it all started. At first I just spoke to the staff, identified the geezer – one time it was a girl – and then I stayed in the background. Bit by bit I got more involved. Patricia says, 'why don't you introduce me?', so we worked out what I should say, and I started doing that. Then she had me giving out cards at the end. I says to Annie, 'it's like I've got a new lease of life. People know me now'.

Like I say, I've been drinking there for nearly 20 years, but I was never good at getting into company. But Patricia started doing a lot of do's there after that so, people got to know me and soon when I went in for a quiet pint it was, 'come and have one with us Archie'.

Poor old Nell was in the corner on her own. I still clapped her plenty though. Good old Nell.

When I got home one night Annie says, 'her next door was in. She comes to the door and says, 'I just popped in for a wee blether Annie.'

She's lived next door for nearly seven years, she's never popped in before.

Annie says, 'then she starts hinting that you are getting awfully friendly with Patricia'.

They work together', my Annie said, 'why wouldn't they be friendly?'

'Your Archie must be about 70 odd now, is he no?', she says.

'My Archie isn't even 64 yet' she said.

'Still, a bit auld to be hanging around with a wee lassie of 22 is he no?', she goes.

'I was fuming', Annie says, 'but I wasn't going to give her the satisfaction. Is there anything going on Archie?', she asked me.

I was floored. 'Annie, what are you thinking? I have no interest in Patricia like that. She's like a wee daughter to me and it's given me a new lease of life, being a minder. I don't really do anything, but I am happy Annie, I'm enjoying it.',

'I know you are Archie, it's great to see it, it's taken you out of yourself', she said.

'Never mind that loudmouth next door, I says.

Annie says, 'She said all the neighbours are talking Annie, that's why I thought it my duty to come and tell you'.

'Annie', I telt her, 'we've known these neighbours for years, nobody's talking. But if you want me to stop it I will. I'll phone Patricia straight away'.

But Annie says, 'no, Archie, don't do that'.

I could see it was playing on her mind though that people might be getting the wrong idea.

Then there was Deek. Our Tommy died young; he didn't quite make it to 22. But he did have Deek. Born three months after Tommy's death. The wee lassie doesn't want anything to do with our side. We don't know why, don't know what went on between them. But I heard wee Deek had started school, so on a Tuesday, after I'd get the pension and the shopping, I'd come home by way of the school in the hope that I might see him.

The first time I saw him was a shock. He's the spitting image of our Tommy. It was like stepping back in time, his wee freckled face, all full of laughter. I wish we'd been able to keep that wee face laughing, but it was the drugs, and our Tommy, he was just another one in a long list of casualties.

Me and Annie had given up the idea of a family, thought it was never going to happen for us, then, after 20 years of marriage, at almost 42 years old I became a daddy. The house was full of noise, and mess and music and laughter. For almost 22 years.

A few times wee Deek was standing near the railings, and I'd have a wee blether with him. Ask him if he was the best runner in the school. He says he was. Ask him if they still taught maths and if they did I would write to my MP; you know just daft things. And I'd come home and tell it all to Annie.

She'd say, 'tell me again Archie, what did he say?', and we'd relive it over and over.

And that's everything, that's all there is to it officer, I tell him'

And he leans forward, leering and says for the umpteenth time, 'now, tell me it all again'.

You see, it was all down to her next door. The loudmouth. She reported me. Says I was a pimp, I had strippers working for me and that I was a paedophile; she'd seen me hanging around the school. Says I was trying to groom wee Deek.

Police picked me up outside the school, kept me at the station overnight. They brought Annie in and questioned her too.

Deek's mother took him out of that school. Me and Annie, we knew we'd never see that boy again.

Then I came home one afternoon, and as soon as I saw Annie I knew. Heart attack. Couldn't take the strain. It had been all over the papers. Pictures of me with Patricia, her in her tassels and me in my best suit, along with a picture of me standing outside the school watching the wean. Even I thought I looked like a paedophile.

Patricia, she had to move to London. For anonymity.

Now I sit here, just back from the window, looking out, wondering what's happening down the Loch Inn. Some people were never sure afterwards. Is he, isn't he? I couldn't bear the sideways glances.

'Men need to talk', it says on the ads on TV nowadays. But who do I talk to? Meanwhile I often hear her next door, leaning on her gate, laughing like a drain, saying, 'aye, you know me, I love a wee blether.'

WHAT???!!! - Ellen Kerr

Johnny Delaney - Sheryll Martin

Lucky Girl Am I - Sheryll Martin

WHAT ???!!!

By Ellen Kerr

What do you have to do
To get someone to listen to you?
WTF!!!! you know what I mean
I promise to keep my language clean

An answer to a query is all I request
But my temperature's rising
And i'm doing my best

The teceptionist at the doc's
Is an arrogant bint
I really want to go down
And give her a dunt !!

Why do they think
It's their right to know
"I want to speak to the doctor
You so and so!!!

A 30 second phone call
Or an expensive appointment
I know what I'd choose
DON'T take me on wummin!
Cause you'll only lose

My blood pressure's rising
I'm gonnae explode
It's all down to you
You stupid old toad !!

LISTEN TO ME
It's all that i'm asking
A simple phone call
Will answer my question

Instead i've gone
From zero to sixty
In no time at all
And all for the sake
Of a SIMPLE PHONE CALL!!!!!

JOHNNY DELANEY

An original poem by Sheryll Martin

We saw his mother cry
As Johnny Delaney
Marched on by
Carrying his duffle bag
Young and with
a confident swag
It's what we all saw
When Johnny Delaney
Went off to war....

His Daddy stood by
Shaking his head
As he recalled
All the young dead
From times before
When boys
Marched off to war
And came back broken
With things
Left unspoken

His brother sad
Did not even understand
The hurried hug
The shook hand
Don't go Johnny
He whispered in vain
As Johnny moved onward
To catch his plane...

God bless you son
His grandpa said

Sleep with one eye open
Keep your helmet on yer head
And promise me
You won't come back dead
But if you do
Know that me and country
Will be proud of you

Jonny Delaney's war
Was in another country
On a distant shore
Somewhere he'd
never been before
Two long long years
Gunfire ringing in his ears
And so much sand
When a bomb took
His leg and then his hand

He came back home
Less than he went
A man with fears
Nightmares and tears
And totally spent
He never laughed
Or smiled again
Never could control
The terrible pain
Without a bottle
In his good hand
And drugs that
Helped him in
His home land
He never again
stood tall
For Johnny Delaney
At 21 had given

His country his all

LUCKY GIRL AM I

An original poem by Sheryll Martin

I was born on British sod
To love my country and my God
Give respect to our royal Queen
And take care of England's green
To feel deep inside
A sense of British pride
When the union jack
Is flown high
As a standard in the sky
I was taught
Freedom was bought
By the young and brave
Carrying our flag to their grave
lay poppies blood red
At the feet of soldiers dead
red white and blue
We love you
And wave
In proud jubilee
Oh my country I vow to thee

But I stand to
Before another flag
Also red white and blue
For a country who
Adopted me
Shared it's bounty
And sweet liberty
Oh I love old glory
Where I live

A brand new story
stars and stripes fly
As a standard In the sky
On uniforms
And coffins draped
War here not escaped
Folded in a widow's hand
A flag that flies
In the skies for
For all to see
What makes us free
Oh my country
Of sweet liberty

So when I stand
And raise my hand
Two powerful flags
Wave over me
How lucky can one girl be?

Secret Star - Lucy A Levason

SECRET STAR

By Lucy A Levason

I want to hang a star for you

Up high

Small

Discreet

One to hide among the thousands

But this one is ours

Everyone can see it

But only we know

So before you go to bed at night

You know...

About the Author

John FR Munro is a writer and poet based in Glasgow, Scotland. He is the founder and treasurer of the Gorbals Writing Group, where he supports, encourages and inspires new writers to take their hobby from procrastination to publication. He is a former member of HM Armed Forces and is currently a Registrar with Glasgow City Council. It was during his childhood in the 50s and 60s that John began to write; when tv and social media were less prevalent. They were no more prevalent in the Army, where reading and writing were considered vital pastimes.

John's influences include Enid Blyton, Arthur Conan Doyle and he is particularly fond of the West Wing writing team. John is currently working on a number of projects, including a book of children's stories for his grandkids, adult crime thriller stories and a television script.

Printed in Great
Britain
by Amazon